For Cameron and Patrick, my little earth-savers.

Love always,
– Mom

Para mi Madre Perla y Rex (for my parents).

With all my love and gratitude,
– E.C.

Santa
Goes
Green

Written by Anne Margaret Lewis  Illustrated by Elisa Chavarri

Mackinac Island Press
for the love of reading

Dear Santa,

My name is Finn. I'm a boy you deliver toys to. I don't mean to seem ungrateful Santa, but I really don't need any more toys.

I have a problem that I need help with instead. Because I am just one boy, in one house, in one town, I'm not sure how to make the world listen to me.

I figured you being Santa and all, you could help me. You seem like a pretty powerful guy.

Thank you for
adopting:

Leopold

CERTIFICAT
OF
ADOPTION

r: Leopold

as.
ad.
n to
I guy.

opold.
anger
out the
g to you.

this year,
his home.
I'm sorry to
e in your
t it's really
listen, or care.
yes Santa.

Elm Street

You see, it's like this Santa. I've adopted a polar bear named Leopold. He is in danger of losing his home. I'm sure you being in the North Pole, you know about the melting glaciers.

All I want this year Santa, is to save Leopold and his home. The glaciers are melting too fast and Leopold needs the sea ice from them to hunt for food. I'm sorry to bother you with this at such a busy time, you know Christmas and all, but this is really important to me. Everyone else is too busy to listen, or care.

I hope you say yes Santa.

Your friend,
Finn

P.S. I'm the 7-year-old boy with red hair on Elm Street.

Finn finished his letter. He tucked a picture of Leopold inside and sealed the envelope closed with a polar bear sticker. At last he rushed off to the mailbox. Santa was his only hope.

Many, many miles away at the North Pole, Santa received letter after letter from children all over the world. He was sitting in his cozy cottage opening them when one slid out of the stack and fell to the floor. He noticed it had a sticker on it. Santa gently placed his spectacles on his droll little nose.

What, this boy wants NO toys for Christmas? he thought to himself.

When he finished reading the polar-bear-stickered letter, he knew he had to talk to this boy with red hair named Finn.

Swift!

Santa called out to his head elf.

"Swift!" he bellowed. "I must talk to this boy named Finn. What's happening with this polar bear named Leopold? And why is all the ice melting?"

"I don't know Santa," said Swift. "But we don't have time for this! Christmas is in just three days." He held up the Countdown-'Til-Christmas pocket watch that Santa had given him and all the other elves.

Santa chuckled and said, "Swift…we will make time."

Swift dashed off to the Santamaphone. He told the elves in the Reindeer Lodge to harness up Santa's Sleigh. They would journey to see Finn.

Worried about Leopold and the melting ice, Santa climbed aboard the sleigh with Swift at his side. Swift was more worried about the Countdown-'Til-Christmas than saving some silly polar bear.

"Why is this polar bear any concern of ours?" asked Swift. "It doesn't have anything to do with Christmas. And what difference can we make? We're just toy makers."

"Finn's hope and belief in me, Swift, has everything to do with Christmas. If Finn needs help saving Leopold, well then, that's exactly what we shall do." Santa wrapped his arm around Swift with a warm tuck.

Their take-off was smooth, but it was still daylight, so they would need to be careful *not* to be seen.

Hearing the jingle from the sky, Finn charged outside.

As Santa stepped out of the sleigh, Finn greeted the big red softy with a giant bear hug.

"I knew it. I knew you wouldn't let me down, Santa."

With Finn's letter tucked safely in his pocket, Santa chuckled. "Ho, Ho, Ho. Now, now, Finn, what's this I hear about you not wanting any toys this year?"

"It's Leopold, Santa," Finn's excited face became serious. "His home is melting and he needs our help. If you take me with you, I can help you find him."

Swift gave Santa a stern look, pointing his tiny finger to his pocket watch. "Christmas, Santa, Christmas!"

They climbed aboard Santa's sleigh. Santa gave a quick jingle of the bells and the reindeer leaped two-by-two into the blue of day.

Santa admired the splendor of the world as they began their quest to save Leopold. But he couldn't help but notice that the world looked *very* different during the day.

The sleigh landed on an iceberg when Finn spotted a white figure in the distance.

"It's him!" shouted Finn as he leaped across the ice floes.

"Leopold!" Finn yelled, grinning from ear to ear.

But when Finn reached the great white mound, it was *not* Leopold. It was a very large, snow-covered walrus. And with an untamed shaking, the walrus waggled all of the snow off of himself and onto Finn, knocking him down.

The grumpy old walrus wailed loudly, "I can assure you that I am *no* polar bear. And I haven't seen any in a long time."

Santa apologized to the walrus for disturbing him. Then he helped Finn to his feet and wrapped him with his big red coat.

"We won't stop looking," Santa told him.

The ice creaked and the water bubbled as a deep, wise voice from below their feet emerged, "Excuse me, but you are not standing on an iceberg. We are a pod of beluga whales, and would you kindly get off my head?" The beluga whale continued, "There are no polar bears around here. There's not enough sea ice. The glaciers are melting, don't you know?"

Just then a baby beluga splashed up and grabbed the green tassel from Swift's hat. She plucked it off of his head and swam away in a beluga game. Swift hopped from one beluga to another trying to catch her. Finally, he stumbled and landed smack-dab on a big pile of snow.

That's it, Santa!" Swift said as his rosy cheeks grew rosier, "I'm going back to the North Pole! We have a Christmas to get ready for!"

Disappointed, Finn agreed with Swift. "He's right, Santa, it's too late. You should go back to the toy shop. Christmas can't wait."

Santa reassured Finn, "We will not give up until we've found him."

Just as Swift grabbed his hat in a huff and began to slide down from the large mound, it began to quiver. They all jumped back as this very large snow pile began to rise and shake the snow from itself.

Standing before them was a magnificent polar bear, BIG and BEAUTIFUL.

"Leopold! It's you!" Finn shouted with joy.

Leopold bowed down in front of Finn and they embraced in a nose-to-nose Eskimo kiss.

Santa and Swift stood over them, looking out at the sparse ice floes. Santa was happy he had helped Finn find Leopold, but how would he help slow down the melting of the glaciers and save Leopold's home?

After a moment, Swift's pocket watch chimed the two-days-till-Christmas ring. He pulled it from his pocket and gave a gentle tug on Santa's coat. After seeing how happy Finn and Leopold were, Swift realized how important this journey had become.

"Santa, we still have time," Swift said. "We *can* make a difference!"

They arrived back at the North Pole and Santa had a grand idea. He leaned in toward Swift and told him of his new plan. "We will collect all of the old toys, Swift, and make them new again. We will reuse last year's wrapping paper. And we will harness the great North Pole wind to help power up the toy shop. The more energy we save, the healthier our planet will be. This will help take care of Leopold's home."

He gave a jolly, "Ho, Ho, Ho." He pulled out his own pocket watch and brightly cheered, "Christmas, Swift. Christmas!"

Finn thanked Santa for listening and hugged Leopold tightly. He whispered softly, "One boy, in one house, in one town did make a difference."

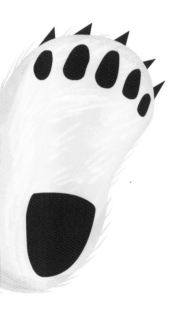

First Edition

Library of Congress Cataloging-in-Publication Data on file
Lewis, Anne Margaret and Elisa Chavarri
Santa Goes Green
Summary: Travel with Finn, a red-haired boy who lives on Elm street, as he enlists the help of Santa on a journey to save a
polar bear and his home—the melting glaciers. Along the way they encounter a walrus and a pod of beluga whales.
Fiction

ISBN 978-1-934133-16-3

10 9 8 7 6 5 4 3 2 1

Printed in USA

Art Direction by Tom Mills
A Mackinac Island Press, Inc. publication
Traverse City, Michigan

www.mackinacislandpress.com

Dear Children of the World,

I want to share some tips on how you can go green. I invite you to visit www.santagoesgreen.org. Swift will be happy to help you with a list of little things we can all do.

Once there, you can also tell me how you are helping to take care of our planet.

Your jolly old elf,

Santa